characters created by l a u r e n

I absolutely MUST do coloring now or painting or drawing

with pictures by

_____

(your name here)

Grosset & Dunlap
An Imprint of Penguin Group (USA) Inc.

Charlie and Lola and Marv and Lotta are taking Sizzles for a walk in the park.

Add more birds...

and butterflies...

and flowers.

Soren Lorensen
is here, too.

Lola seems to be **drawing** a **creature**.

What could it be?

This is Lola's **invisible friend**,
Soren Lorensen.

What would your **invisible friend** look like?

The tree is full of birds, and each one is a different color.

Fill the branches with birds and leaves...

How many more bugs can you draw?

You
could
try using
real
leaves.

Marv is walking his dog, Sizzles.

What's that on the end of Lotta's leash?

Is it a **dog**, or something much, much **bigger**?

Lola is wearing her winter scarf. Can you make it very extremely long?

Lotta would like to wear a **princess crown.**

Lola is wearing an ever so very tall hat.

What's **that** on Soren Lorensen's head?

Marv's hat is extremely silly!

Charlie would really like a feather in his hat. Perhaps you could use a real one.

Lola has invited a **martian** over for tea and he's **drinking** her pink milk through **one** of his mouths.

What are his **three** long **arms** reaching for?

What has Lola left on her **plate**?

What do you think **martians** eat?

Try cutting pictures of food out of magazines.

Charlie is eating messy spaghetti...

Lola says, "Look at that, Charlie, isn't it **strange**?"

What do **you** think Charlie and Lola are looking at?

Lola is **waving** from the **window**.

Who could be waving from the other **windows**? Marv, Lotta, or maybe it's **you**.

Lola is helping Charlie build
a really **tall rocket** for school,

but they need your help.

Try cutting and pasting, too.

Lola is planet-jumping onto . . .

ever so sparkly . . .

really very spotty . . . .

completely stripy planets.

Lola is wearing her **favorite** and her best **dress**.

What **pattern** do you think it could be?

Try using real **material**.

Does it have **buttons**? Or a **zipper**?

Or cut something out from a **magazine**.

What
do you
think
Charlie is
standing
on?

Is it a **box**,
or a **chair**,
or maybe even
an **elephant**?

What is Lola running away from?

This is what Charlie looks like
when he's **happy**.

What do you think he looks like when
he's making a **funny face**...

or **embarrassed**...

or **cross**?

What does Lola look like
when she's **thinking**...

or when she's **sad**...

or **singing**...

or really very **sleepy**?

Lola is dreaming about what the tooth fairy will bring...

Good night,
Lola.